WOMANIYA: THE CURLY TALES OF HER

ARCHANA SINGH

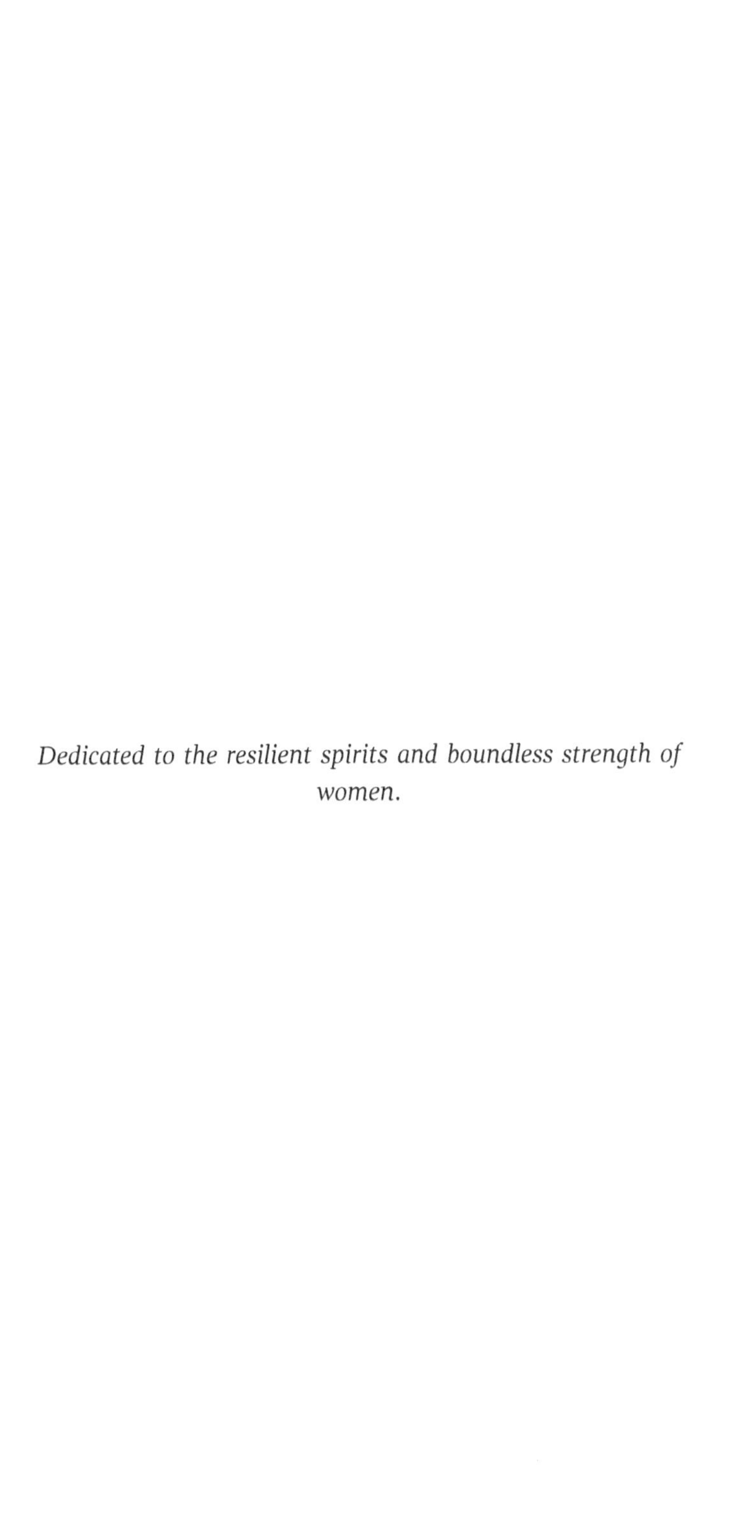

Dedicated to the resilient spirits and boundless strength of women.

Contents

Foreword

This is a fine collection of short stories that explore women's battles with narrow social expectations and systemic injustice in the Indian cultural milieu. It beautifully narrates tales of women who live around us, real beings, not phantoms; their quiet heroism of everyday survival in a moral universe that contains little space for them to sprawl, chipping away every moment at their agency, their will. As we get up close with the protagonists of these tales, we, the readers, recognize our own making (or unmaking?), the gender codes that consume us, and the way forward, fraught with battles with our own corrupt selves to retrieve finally the real 'self', however drowsy and haggard, hidden beneath layers of the burden of lies.

Dr. Suraj Gunwant
Department of English
Ewing Christian College, Prayagraj

Preface

"Womaniya: The Curly Tales of Her" is a captivating collection of stories celebrating women's diverse and intricate experiences from various walks of life. The book is a canvas of narratives, each highlighting the female spirit's strength, resilience, and uniqueness. From tales of empowerment and self-discovery to stories of overcoming challenges and breaking societal norms, this book offers a glimpse into the lives of women who refuse to be confined by expectations. Whether it's a young woman navigating her career in a male-dominated industry, a mother balancing her dreams with familial responsibilities, or a woman from a marginalized community asserting her voice, each story sheds light on the multifaceted nature of womanhood.

"Womaniya: The Curly Tales of Her" is a tribute to the boundless potential and indomitable spirit that resides within every woman, inspiring readers to embrace their journey with courage and grace. Though partly fictionalized, this riveting book is based on true stories. Few of the stories have occupied their place in "The Criterion: An International Journal in English".

I would like to express my gratitude to all those who accidentally become a part of my life and appreciate their support in providing a window to sneak peek into their life for a magnifying view.

Dr. Archana Singh

Motherhood: An Eternal Bliss

"Oh my God! I am getting wet ...What's this? Call the doctor immediately. Where is the bag to be taken? Get the money from almirah. Let me call Bhabhi first, as she has been continuously reviewing my medical reports." I groaned.

"It's 10:30 PM, its late she might be slept," replied Arnav

No, let me call her, she is a doctor. I looked into the perplexed eyes of my mother and told her to get ready to come with me. With my sinking heart I picked my phone to call my Bhabhi, a doctor in Faridabad. Her Phone is ringing ...come on pick up the phone, somewhere I am in hurry. "Yes, she picked." I cried, "Bhabhi! Bhabhi! My clothes are getting wet and I am not able to control that liquid. I went to the washroom but of no use."

"When did you get your last ultrasound done?" asked Bhabhi.

"Today itself, and the doctor said, "Don't worry everything is fine, you have to wait for a few more days," I replied. I can sense the urgency in her voice while talking. "Your water bag is leaked. Meet your doctor immediately and rush to the hospital. Don't worry I am coming and meet you soon. Bye, take care," she instructed me. There is a pin-drop silence in my room and the weather outside is in a different mood. Strong wind is blowing with a whistling sound, trees are shaking their branches making ghostly noise. Arrae! Arrae! What happened to electricity now, shouted mummy while packing the bag, and Arnav speedily entered my room and in a shaky voice said, "The doctor asked us to meet her at her residence, let us meet her immediately." I started crying ...with a tense and confused mind, I sat in a car. "Mummy, have you kept everything that was mentioned in the list?" I enquired her. "Yes! I have kept, you don't worry, keep yourself calm," she said. It was 11 PM some of the neighbours were preparing their beddings and making their kids sleep while some were still strolling in the park enjoying the weather. The thoroughfare with trees on both sides, was unknown to me and resembled a long snake in a forest. "Seat is also wet now," I whisper in Arnav's ear. "Don't worry, we have reached the doctor's residence," consoled Arnav. After the examination doctor instructed us to immediately reach the hospital, she had already informed the hospital and would be there in 20 minutes. "It's raining!!!!, I cried. "You have to go by car then why are you taking tension," he replied angrily. We reached the hospital at 12AM, staff was ready to receive me, as they were already informed by the doctor. I was nervous and my heart was sinking and I could see only a few people in the hospital as it was midnight. Two nurses took me to a room in a wheelchair and removed all my jewellery and the auspicious red thread tied on my left hand. Now I had only a knee length gown on my body open from the back and I was feeling embarrassed. My doctor entered the room and asked the nurse about a senior doctor who had to give anesthesia to me. My lips started chanting *Hanuman Chalisa* and other religious hymns and I noticed a urine bag connected to my body as a piece of costume jewellery. Nurses took me into a room equipped with machines with a bed at the centre. Doctor asked me to lie down on that bed, and started discussing with the other doctors about my case. Suddenly a very old man with white grey hair entered the room. He took my reports in his hand and started preparing an injection for me. While he was busy in measuring the dosage, nurses were beautifying me with different machines to check my blood pressure; my heartbeat, and an oxygen mask to check my breathing. The moment I saw the old man coming towards me with a syringe, my heartbeat increased the pace and my lips started chanting mantras that were coming to my mind at that time. "Sit slowly, I will give you this injection so that your lower part of the body is anesthetized. It will be like an ant bite, but don't move while I'm injecting," said the doctor. My lips were seized and I sat as directed by him. He injected the medicine and rubbed the point with a cotton swab. "Now lie down slowly," his relaxed voice commanded me. His voice comforted me; I was assured that everything was going fine and under control. My doctor started hitting my feet with a hammer to check the senses. "I still can sense, don't cut," I replied with tears in my eyes, my body started feeling cold and needed warmth suddenly a sound came Pllkkkcchhhh! My doctor was on her task and I could sense the movement of hands, but everything was blurred for me; suddenly I saw a big red ball with black hair in her hand, and that ball started crying very loudly. The doctor's team increased the speed, I could hear...scissors! thread! Cotton! Check BP! it's a boy, you are mommy congratulations! I lost my senses. When I opened my eyes, I was in a different and quiet room, but this time in a full green gown. Arnav entered the room; he sat beside me and low down to look into my eyes; his fingers moved on my oily hair. "How are you? Everything is fine, we are blessed with a brave boy, *Arjun*. It's drizzling out and Bhabhi reached the hospital when you were in the operation theatre," said Arnav in a very excited voice. He put his passionate lips on my cheeks. "Congratulations!" I replied with a spark in my eyes, the spark of motherhood. Yes, I am a blessed mother with a 24*7 job of loving, caring, and playing with my *Arjun*

The Fragrance of Love

"How can I stay away from you?" cried Ria and started weeping against Raj's chest. Raj put his hands around her and kissed her forehead with tears in his eyes.

"You are my strong girl, don't cry, we can manage the situation."

Raj and Ria got married in the year 2005. Though being from the same caste Raj's family was not ready to accept Ria as their daughter-in-law. Raj was determined to have Ria in his life. After facing a lot of issues in their family, they convinced their families and became one soul on 4 Dec 2005. They got what they had dreamt of. On October 4, they were blessed with a son, Arjun, who completed them and made their world blissful. They both were happy in their profession, but at some point, they realized that they should try for a government job to have steadiness in their later years of life. They both started filling out forms. Raj's keen eyes were always on the employment newspaper.

"Ria there are vacancies in your field in engineering colleges, the job you were dreaming of".

"What about the vacancy in your field?" inquired Ria.

Raj: Yes, I will also apply and hope that at least one of us can get the job.

Both of them filled out the forms and appeared for the written test. Fifteen days later, while having tea in the evening, "This is an unknown number I will not pick up the call. Students have developed the tendency of calling on off days", Ria murmured in irritation as she was with Raj.

The phone rings again, showing the same number. Ria, in irritation, picks up the phone and gets shocked. The call is from one of the engineering colleges confirming the interview. She got excited and hugged Raj. "You will also soon receive a call".

Time passed, and Raj did not receive any call but was very happy as Ria got a chance to prove her capability. Since the time was very short to make all the necessary arrangements, they thought leaving a small child alone at home with anyone, even temporarily, could be concerning and potentially risky. Above all, Arjun, being very naughty, could not be left with anybody in the home, so they decided to take him along with them. Raj said, "We will go by flight, it saves our time".

Ria: No, never...flight... I would prefer to die rather than go by flight.

Somehow, Raj convinced Ria, and the day came when they had to board a flight. "I have kept cotton balls and orange candies to control the ear pressure". She nervously said. Being alert during every process of her boarding, her heart was thumping at the highest pace. She boards the airbus and starts chanting prayers. It took around one hour for them to reach Lucknow from Delhi. Raj kept on telling Ria to be confident and give her best. The day came 29 November, Raj's birthday. Ria gave her interview and was optimistic about her selection as she gave her best, and it was her lucky day...her Raj came into this world. After the interview, they decided to celebrate the day. They went to the Zoo as Arjun was fond of birds and animals. His sparkling eyes scanned every bird and animal. Trio went for candlelight dinner to make the day more special and cherished every moment they spent on that special day. They came back to Delhi eagerly waiting for the result. After one week,

Bip! Bip! Ria's mobile rings twice, an indication of the incoming message.

"It's a message from the university," screamed Ria. Raj snatched the mobile from Ria's hand and read the message, "They have asked to collect the joining letter after two days from Lucknow".

With a fumbling voice and tears in their eyes, Ria shrank in Raj's arms. She has to reach Lucknow on the 7th of December. They made all the necessary arrangements and reached Lucknow. The sweet dream they saw was about to be fulfilled, but the moment they came to know that Ria had to join on that very day and the posting was 750 km away from Raj, it became a nightmare. They were not able to accept reality.

Somehow, Ria accepted the offer and requested the director to permit her to join the college after two days, as she had to make all the necessary arrangements for her baby and Raj. With a heavy heart, Raj and Ria made all the arrangements, but both of them were not ready to accept that they would live away from each other. While packing her bag, her tears were rolling out, and in the other room, Raj was trying to control his emotions but could not stop his tears. They tightly hugged each other and wept. Raj accompanied Ria to her college in Banda. She has to stay in a hostel, away from her family. Luck has twisted their lives. In the evening, Raj left Ria and went back to Delhi. Now Raj has to take care of Arjun and himself. It's now been four months. Raj has learned a lot of things. He prepares food for Arjun and makes him ready for school. Ria, on the other hand, travels every week to meet her little world. Raj sometimes gets irritated and shows his anger through anti-love messages, but their love is so deep ...so true that in anger also, one can feel the fragrance of love.

Appraisal

This government Engineering College of Uttar Pradesh was a three-storey structure, painted in a cool shade of white, with accents of grey on the windowsills and ridges with beautiful aluminium door frames. It was situated on a tree-lined avenue, flanked by lush green Gul mohar and palm trees, providing much-needed shade in the scorching Indian summers. As the students and faculty entered through the main gate, they were greeted by the sight of the college's emblem proudly displayed above the entrance, a symbol of knowledge and progress. There worked a diligent and dedicated government employee named Dr. Anjana. She was known for her commitment to her job and her unwavering principles. Anjana was employed in the Department of Applied Science and Humanities.

Dr. Anjana joined the Department of Applied Science and Humanities with great enthusiasm and a strong commitment to her work. Her dedication to upholding the highest standards of education and research was well-known among her colleagues. However, trouble began to brew soon after her arrival, as she found herself in a challenging situation with her immediate boss, Dr. B.D.

Dr. B.D. had been in charge of the department's Induction Program, a prestigious responsibility that involved welcoming new students and ensuring their smooth integration into the academic environment. However, as Dr. B.D. was a deceitful person, he decided to pass on some of his responsibilities to Dr. Anjana. One day, Dr. B.D. approached her and asked her to take over a significant portion, i.e., sightseeing and local tours for new students of the Induction Program. He claimed that it was an excellent opportunity for her to showcase her leadership skills and gain recognition within the department. However, Dr. Anjana, being a meticulous person, had several questions about the logistics and responsibilities involved in managing the program effectively.

As she probed deeper and sought clarification on the specifics, Dr. B.D. grew increasingly uncomfortable. It became apparent that he couldn't provide clear answers to her questions. Dr. Anjana's commitment to transparency and accountability made her unwilling to accept vague instructions, especially when they concerned a crucial program like the Induction Program.

Frustrated by Dr. Anjana's reluctance to comply with his unclear directives, Dr. B.D. resorted to a darker path. He began to exert pressure on her, subtly at first, and then overtly. He hinted that her ACR (Annual Confidential Report), a critical document that influenced her career progression, could be adversely affected if she did not comply with his demands.

She felt trapped and conflicted. She knew that compromising her principles to please Dr. B.D. was not the right path, but the threat to her career weighed heavily on her mind. She confided in a trusted colleague, who encouraged her to document the incidents and seek guidance from the higher authorities of the institute.

Summoning her courage, she decided to take a stand against Dr. B.D.'s unethical behaviour. She reported the situation to the director of the institute and also filed a complaint with the ICC (Internal Compliant Committee). The authorities launched an investigation into the matter.

As the investigation into Dr. B.D.'s actions continued to unfold, it became abundantly clear that he had indeed attempted to misuse his authority and had behaved inappropriately toward Dr. Anjana. The evidence was compelling, and it left no room for doubt regarding his misconduct.

In light of these findings, disciplinary action was deemed necessary, and the committee recommended the director of the institute to issue a formal notice to Dr. B.D. However, a troubling twist emerged, the copy of the notice was not marked to the committee (ICC) that recommended action against Dr. B.D.

This omission raised serious concerns about the integrity and transparency of the internal authorities. It suggested that there might be an effort to shield Dr. B.D. from the full consequences of his actions. By withholding the notice from the ICC, the authorities effectively circumvented the committee's role in overseeing the disciplinary process.

Even more disconcerting was that the notice was not shared with the complainant, Dr. Anjana, who had bravely come forward to report the misconduct in the first place. This lack of transparency and communication left her in the dark regarding the progress and outcome of the disciplinary proceedings against Dr B.D., denying her the right to be informed and to participate in the process as a concerned party.

This situation raised serious questions about the institution's commitment to addressing workplace harassment and misconduct. It became evident that there was a pressing need for greater accountability, transparency, and adherence to established protocols to ensure that victims of harassment, like Dr. Anjana, received the justice and support they deserved.

II

Time passed and now came the time to submit the annual confidential report for appraisal. Dr. Anjana had submitted her meticulously prepared annual confidential report to the Department of Applied Science and Humanities with a sense of accomplishment. Her report was a testament to her hard work and dedication, showcasing her outstanding performance in research, teaching, and various other activities. However, her apprehension about Dr. B.D.'s intentions proved to be well-founded when Dr. B.D. did not forward her report to the director and returned her report. It was as though he had unleashed a storm of queries and criticisms upon it. Each page was filled with his red ink, questioning her achievements, research contributions, and even her teaching methodology. It was clear that Dr. B.D. was going to great lengths to find faults in her work. Dr. Anjana felt like she was walking on eggshells as she reviewed Dr. B.D.'s comments. The weight of his scrutiny was heavy, and she began to doubt her own abilities. She knew that her report was strong and deserved recognition, but Dr. B.D.'s actions were indicating something different.

As the department's annual performance evaluations were announced, a cloud of anxiety hung over Dr. Anjana. She couldn't help but fear the worst, especially considering the relentless scrutiny and critical comments on her report. When the results were finally posted, her heart sank. The entire department, including Dr. B.D., had been marked "outstanding" in their annual evaluations. However, despite her impeccable record and the highest marks in research and other activities, Dr. Anjana had been rated as "very good." It was a glaring discrepancy that left her feeling bewildered and outraged. She knew that this was not a fair reflection of her contributions and capabilities. It was evident that Dr. B.D.'s personal bias and ill intentions had influenced her evaluation. She felt betrayed by the very system she had trusted to recognize and reward her hard work and dedication.

On that tranquil night when the full moon cast its silvery glow upon the world, she found herself ensnared in the labyrinthine recesses of her own mind. The night was painted in shades of silver, as the moon hung high in the star-studded canvas of the sky. Its radiant beams filtered through the curtains, casting ethereal shadows in her dimly lit room. Outside, the world seemed to be bathed in a serene, mystical light, as if nature itself was trying to soothe the turmoil within her. Her mind was not accepting the injustice done to her; tears were rolling out making her eyes red and swollen. The lines etched upon her features seemed to narrate a story of relentless stress and inner conflict.

She was abruptly awakened from this horrifying and upsetting dream, her heartbeat was thumping as the nightmare's memories clung to her memory. Her anxiety was intuitive because it had seemed so real to her. Dr. B.D., the name that had followed her in her dream, lingered in her mind like an ominous shadow. She couldn't help but sense that the dream might have a deeper meaning as the dream's fragments slowly faded away. It appeared as though her unconscious mind was trying to warn her, pleading with her to take precautions to defend herself from a potential danger. She came to the conclusion that she needed to pay attention to her instincts and intuition. Despite being terrifying, the dream may be a sign. The next day, following her unsettling dream and driven by her commitment to fairness and improvement, she took decisive action. She submitted an application through the proper channels to request access to her Annual Confidential Report (ACR). Her intention was clear: to provide employees with an opportunity to review their reports and identify areas where they could improve in their respective fields. However, her move created a whirlwind of controversy within the administration. The officials staunchly resisted her request, citing the confidential nature of the reports and asserting that they should not be disclosed. Behind this resistance, a darker motive emerged – it became evident that some were using the confidentiality of the ACRs as a means to manipulate and harass employees. The threat of spoiling an employee's ACR was being exercised as a tool to maintain control over employees.

As the tension escalated, the matter was finally taken to the college's Board of Governors (BOG), the highest decision-making authority. Dr. Anjana ransacked countless court orders and legal precedents to find a solid legal foundation for her request. Each search was a battle for her. She sensed hope when she stumbled upon a Supreme Court document that supported her cause. Armed with a Supreme Court order that she had found during her research, Dr. Anjana presented her case before the BOG with unwavering conviction. The Supreme Court order supported her argument for transparency and fairness. After careful consideration of the legal implications and the principle of transparency, the BOG made a landmark decision in favour of Dr. Anjana. It was a resounding victory, not only for her but for all the employees who had been subjected to the unfair practices and manipulations surrounding their ACRs. The decision signalled a shift towards a more equitable and just system within the institution.

A Friend or a Freak

"I am on forced medical leave...
I don't want to see him because his over-possessiveness is impairing my mental state".
I was appointed as an Assistant Professor in a government organization. I was staying away from my family. Staying alone does not mean I shall give up in front of wrongdoers. God has drawn a lot of challenging lines in my hand. I have been given the posting almost 600 kilometres away from my home, away from my only son, and above all, in the typical male-dominated office and chauvinistic environment. The start of my new journey in a government organization with new faces, different work cultures, and so-called caring people could have been fascinating. Everything in the office seemed to be peripherally normal, but coequality was absent. After two months, I started sensing the wrong vibes from some people, especially my Head of the Department (HoD). He was a middle-aged man with a short height and almost

bald head with a bald mind. He used to pretend to be an intensive caring and helping man. It seemed as if he was my inborn enemy. I still remember his favourite line for me, "You visit your home, I will manage here, and you put your signature in the register after returning… write an application, and I will tear it once you return….it means no official record of leave", but later I came to know that he used to go to his home without taking leave and put his signature in the register. Such a lovely enemy I got…

Our head-on collision was first reported in February, and that too on 14 February. He came into my cabin after office hours and started shouting; by chance, my two colleagues were there with me in my office cabin. The matter was reported to the Director, and a committee was formed to investigate the case. The investigation seemed biased, but my (male) colleague Dr. Ram Tripathi, who was present at the time of the incident in my cabin, gave his honest statement. The committee members, especially women, took me to a room and tried to make me understand that these things happen in every organization and you should take your steps back. My father used to tell me, "Don't bow in front of the wrong people and wrong-doers." I didn't look back and asked the ladies to proceed with my case. I mentioned a male colleague in the above lines just to reiterate that all men are not mean and cheap like others in my department. Even after three years, the case was pending as I didn't receive any letter from the committee except the information that the committee recommended the Director to issue a warning letter to my HoD for his wrong behaviour.

This love of my enemy did not end up here only. His blocked and pig head started plotting different levels of problems for me.

During that chaos, almost one and half years back, I met a social worker, Vishal, who helped me resolve some of my office problems. Soon, we started chatting, sharing, and caring. He used to share his childhood days and his medical conditions. He seemed to be a simple and nation lover who was always ready to help needy people. Time passed, but through some of the incidents and his confession, I came to know that he is an alcoholic and chain smoker. I was emotionally attached to him, wanting him to give up drinking and smoking. I had always seen his good side, but now I can sense a negative side of his mind. Many a time, I stopped talking with him and blocked his number but resumed talking to him as he used to play with my mind and was in continuous touch with me. One day, he told me that he needed to meet a psychiatrist. He felt that he had a dual personality, and again, I thought I should be with him. He often showered a lot of kindness and motivated me, "You are a strong lady who knows how to manage family and professional life."

In the midst of understanding Vishal's mind and his problem, I landed up in another trouble plotted by HoD. HoD was now ready with his arms and ammunition. He was back with his wicked team. The team was made up of people who were unfairly benefitted by HoD and the director. Vishal assured me, "If you are right, go ahead." He tried to help me in the best possible way he could.

I took a very strong decision to fight the wrongdoers legally and filed a complaint in Mahila Aayog to get justice. On the other hand, Vishal's socio-political career was wambling due to his extremist behaviour and alcoholic habits. I took a leave from the office to rejuvenate my mind and tried to find solace at my home. My family knew about Vishal, but I had not informed them about his extremist behaviour. This time, my family came with me to provide me with moral support and a cool environment. We were happily living, but then Vishal came to stay with us. He told me that he would help me in fighting for justice. For almost 12 days he stayed with us and thought of going to Prayagraj to meet his friends. We went to drop him at Prayagraj to ensure he would not return, but after three days, he returned to meet me again. Instead of focusing on my office work, I was trying to understand this maniac.

Vishal used to tell me he respects women, "नारी पूजनीय है, मैं हर नारी का सम्मान करता हूँ." In public, he was polite with everyone and over-polite with ladies, but this time, he was shouting at me even if I was opening my mouth. I came to know that he was a distant relative of my HoD and HoD went to meet him at his house. I was confused about whether the change in Vishal's behaviour was due to his budding relationship with HoD or something else.

Suddenly, my husband had to leave for his office work; my son and I were alone at home. For the first time, we both had a strange feeling in the presence of Vishal. He started consuming alcohol before coming for dinner and used to stay in our room all night ...shouting at my son, "Sleep otherwise, I will break your laptop...I will kidnap you if you don't listen to me."

He did not allow him to call my husband and asked him to show him his phone. He checked his call details. We became captive in our own house. Those two days were like a nightmare that we had not dreamt of. It seemed there was no blood in our veins because we both were speechless and were trying to console each other through the corners of our eyes. Vishal behaved as if it were his own house, and we both had to make him feel good. Such strange and unexpected behaviour; my health started deteriorating due to sleepless nights and office pressure. I phoned my husband and requested him to come early, "try to come early; we are not well."

The next morning (the third day), Vishal got calls from his friends and family members asking him to return as his mother was admitted to a hospital last night. I enquired him, "You did not receive calls in the night." He said, "My phone was in silent mode." There were 10-15 calls on his number. He said he had to leave for his home.

Yes, of course! You should! Your mother wants to meet you; you were out for so many days, she must have overthought about your absence, and above all, she is your mother," I tried to console him.

With a trembling heart, I requested him, "Please do not come as she must be thinking wrong about our relationship...not only she but everyone."

No, dear, it is not so, Vishal replied in a very low voice.

Finally, he left for his home, and I came to know that he did not meet his mother. The other day, he called me again to book a guest house for him, which I denied as my husband had not returned yet. Vishal tried to pressurize me; I could sense that he was not in his senses. The next day, he informed my husband that he was on his way to my organization. I had not overcome that two-day trauma and was unprepared to welcome his strange nuisance. We left for our hometown to avoid him, but that inebriated maniac shouted and abused everyone, including me, at the gate of my organization. When he came to his senses, he realized what he had done; he apologized for his doings; still apologizing, BUT he has lost me forever... he was good for me, but I was clueless about what made him do so. His over-possessiveness was impairing my mental health.

Was this a conspiracy to low down my confidence to not fight for my rights? Was this a step to make me mentally unstable? I am still on leave to normalize and energize myself to get back to my work.

How a person that too a female can fight against these academic goons? Justice can be delayed but cannot be denied. I still have strong faith that I can prove how spineless academic managers are plaguing society. No matter how strong they are, I will continue to fight my case alone.

She and Her Fighting Instinct

"Slurp, Slurp!! Ahh, it's relaxing to have a cup of tea after an utterly exhausting day", a thought is dancing in my mind while having a ginger and basil crushed tea. Tring...Tring...my cellphone rings. Oh! Hi! Ma'am, after a long time ...almost after three years, I heard your voice. It's my colleague, Rosy, from my previous institute. "Ma'am, are you free? I have something to tell you." She enquired. Yes ma'am! Always free for you.

Rosy: "Is it the right time to talk to you?"

Rosy: Yes, dear! Of course.

Rosy: Ma'am, I am fed up with my family life and husband. My husband, George, is a trauma for me. We have been together for 11 years with no love or emotional bond. This relationship is a concoction of grief, anger, and disdain and is now engulfing my inner space. To protect the honour and dignity of my family, I could not speak and confront to date, but it is suffocating for me to live with George. He is autistic, and his family secreted this information at the time of our marriage, and now they are not accepting the reality.

Me: Is it? I was under the impression that you had a good family, and even you did not give the hint of this when we were together.

Rosy: It all started 11 years back when I got engaged to George. This marriage proposal was done with the help of his maternal uncle. Initially, his uncle showed a striking appearance of George and his family. But two days before our marriage, he said, "It is your choice for this marriage, and I am not taking any guarantee of the groom." The festive and fanfare of the wedding house suddenly changed into a melancholy situation for my family. All the preparations had been done; invitation cards were distributed, and two days to go before the marriage. How do we confront the situation? I was looking at my parents' traumatic condition. One could see the discolouration/ yellowing of their faces. I, being the only child, decided to marry George. However, if this marriage could not take place, society would assassinate my character and gossip about this shit without knowing the truth. My parents, who were dreaming of my bright and happy married life, would not bear this shock. Moreover, finding a suitable match is difficult once a girl is stigmatized.

The marriage day was not looking the way it should be.

The decoration was there, but none of us was happy. It seemed that God was giving us the clues to stop and rethink. My father tried to encourage me to rethink, but with latent fear somewhere in the corner of my heart, I was consoling myself and thinking the other way around that maybe someone, out of jealousy and hatred, was trying to create a problem in our marriage.

I was dressed in a gleaming gown with no gleam on my face, a beautiful headdress of smiling flowers, but I, with a ponderous heart, was ready to exchange the rings. Through the net veil, I dared to see my husband's face. He seemed normal but was avoiding eye contact with me. Now, we both were married, but that compassionate response from a husband was missing.

In the wee hours of the next day, it was time to bid adieu to my parents. With a heavy heart and tears rolling out of my eyes, I looked into my papa's eyes to assure him everything would be fine. That day, I saw fear on my papa's face; he was hiding his red eyes filled with tears. I reached my in-law's house to begin my new life and to be a part of a new family.

On my first night, like other girls, I had also woven dreams and fancied many things. George entered the room and straight away went to the washroom. I was sitting in a red stone sequenced gown at the corner of the bed. He came out and asked me to sleep as he was too exhausted because of the whole day's rituals. I did not say anything and was still sitting; he, in a loud tone, asked me to sleep without asking anything. I lay down like a withered flower on the bed, thinking of my decision. The next day, we had to leave for Kashmir for our honeymoon. I was shocked to see my mother-in-law was ready with her bags to accompany us on our trip. This was beyond my thought.

The trip was not a honeymoon trip, as only one room was booked in a hotel. It seemed as if there was some insurgency, and I was caged. All my dreams were shattered in two days, for there was no one with whom I could share my inner turmoil. George is the only son; his father died when he was 6 years old. The time passed and I came back to my home; I did not share anything with my parents and kept it to myself to safeguard the reputation of both families.

The days passed, and no love and compassion sparked in my husband's heart. The more I came to know about him, the more I felt alienated. I thought of doing a job to normalize myself as it was a setback and I felt that I could not do anything. But, indeed, there is always a silver of hope, and I got a call from a reputed university in Gurugram. To leave my in-law's house and convince George took me a month, but finally, George and I moved to Gurugram with the condition that every weekend we had to visit my mother-in-law. I happily agreed to the condition as this was a golden opportunity to restart my life. In Gurugram, I felt that my life was moving toward normalization. I started feeling happy, and George was also a little bit changing.

Me: I know it was wonderful working together. Jasleen, you and I used to snack together in the evening. Do you remember how Jasleen used to mimic our department's professors?

Rosy: Ahahah! Yes, I feel nostalgic when I recall those days of our togetherness. Ma'am, it was fine at the office, but again, at home, I could not give wings to myself to live freely and happily.

One day, while returning home, George was driving a car. There was a red light of 60 seconds; the moment the red light changed to green, everyone was in a hurry to move, and in that haste, an auto-rickshaw man came in front of our car. George got so irritated and started honking. George fastened his vehicle, stopped in front of that auto rickshaw, and started yelling at him.

"Gadi ke agae kaise aaye. I will kill you, Bastard.

I knew there was no fault of that auto driver, but he started his auto and tried to escape, but George came back to the car and followed the auto and started hitting the auto. I tried to calm him, and it took me around 15 minutes to calm down. On that day, his anger gave me goosebumps. He reacted abnormally in that situation. After that incident, I found him doing such things occasionally.

Me: Don't be scared. We are here to help you.

Rosy: Ma'am, It was not only this; even in bed, he behaved like a maniac. He said to me, I hate your organs. Maximum time he used to spend in the washroom with his laptop. My heart and mind got derailed. It was like a daily scene in our house. There is a lot to share with you, ma'am. I don't know from where I got this courage after 11 years of my marriage and having a child, Tanu. I feel suffocated and need someone to share and lighten my heart with. Oh! It is time for Tanu's therapy; I will get back to you soon. Thanks for listening to my pain, ma'am.

Me: You can call me anytime. Don't worry, everything will be fine. Take care. Bye.

Part-II

Annu (My Husband): what happened? Why are you so disturbed?

Me: Rosy called me up a few minutes back. She was distressed and anxious to find a solution to her own generated problem. I was told a different story, the opposite of what we had seen when she worked with us.

Annu: Is it?

Me: Her husband is autistic....

Annu: Are you in your senses?

Me: Same was my reaction when Dr. Rosy told me this. She kept quiet and bore everything to veil this from society.

Annu: How is her daughter?

Me: She told me that her husband is unable to perform anything on the bed, and her daughter was born with the help of IVF.

Annu: But you told me she gave birth to a boy a few months ago.

Me: She did not inform me about that.

Annu: This is something very strange. She was quite a brilliant and professional lady with ethics.

Me: Hmm!!! But now, the situation is different; she does not want to continue with her marriage. She tried her best to cope with the situation, but nothing was fruitful.

Annu: You don't worry. Everything will be fine!!

Tringgg...Tringgg....Tringgg Oh, Rosy's call

Me: Hi ma'am...Is everything OK?

Rosy: I just thought of talking to you... I feel light when I speak to you

Me: Hahaha...you are always welcome. How is your daughter doing now?

Rosy: I have personally hired a physiotherapist. He visits on alternate days to treat her.

Me: Great! What about Jimmy, your son

Rosy: He is good but very naughty and can't stay in one place for a second. By God's grace, he is perfectly OK.

Me: God always gives the best to his people. Is Jimmy also an IVF child?

Rosy: No, ma'am...I want to tell you something. Due to troubles in my married life, I came closer to one of my colleagues, James. He stepped forward and tried to understand my trauma. We were in a three-year relationship, and Jimmy was his son.

Me: What are you saying?

Rosy: When I asked him to marry me, he started cooking stories, saying his family would disown him if he married against their wish. He was the person who asked me to divorce my husband, George, as he felt that I deserved a good life. He pretended that he was helping me. But actually, he was using me. I pleaded with him not to spoil Jimmy's life, as George knows he is infertile. Jimmy is not his son, and he is born out of wedlock.

And my fear takes the shape of a reality. George made allegations against me and declared that Jimmy was not his son. In this hustle and bustle, he tried to kill me, but I was rescued by my parents. After many counselling sessions, George and I decided to go for a mutual divorce with the condition that our daughter would stay with her biological father and I would be her custodian until she was 18 years old.

I pleaded with James to marry me, but he denied it. I met his parents and told them their son is having a son with me. They denied everything and said, we cannot accept everyone with whom our son has slept or had an affair". It was a jolt for me, and I decided to take a legal step and teach them a lesson for their misdoings.

I came back and filed a case against James. James laughed at me when his parents supported his act and judged me wrong.

I wrote a letter to the chief minister; immediate action was taken. James was arrested and put behind bars. He has been suspended from his workplace but is on conditional bail. I took this step because he did wrong to me, and if I did nothing to get justice, he would spoil another girl's life. Once the person goes unpunished, he will repeat the same with more courage.

Me: Oh! It's you. I read this news in a newspaper almost a month ago, but names were not mentioned. You are a fighter. People like James repeat the same thing confidently when they do not get punished. You are on a battlefield and should not give up till this guy receives punishment for his misdeed. He has marred your image publicly.

You took the right step at the right time. I always appreciate your audacious nature, and now I have seen it also. Hoping you become an example for all. Good luck ...

Bye and take care.

A Language Tapestry: Interwoven with Love, Compassion, and Perseverance

Once famous for dakoits, Banda was an old-fashioned city surrounded by the Vindhyachal range. Almost 30 km from Banda, a government engineering college was constructed, a place of dreams, aspirations, and discoveries. There was a remarkable English teacher named Ms Anjana Singh. She had a passion for literature and a heart brimming with warmth and compassion. To her, teaching wasn't merely a profession; it was an opportunity to inspire young minds and to knit bonds that would last a lifetime. Ms. Singh believed that education was about imparting knowledge and creating meaningful associates with her students.

Ms. Singh's Language Laboratory was a haven—a tapestry of words and ideas adorning its walls. The students, initially uncertain, soon found themselves immersed in the world of literature and Language. In every session, as they walked into her Language, they felt a sense of excitement and wonder. She had a unique way of weaving stories, breathing life into characters, and making her students see beyond the black and white of textbooks. She prepared her budding engineers to be cognizant of all fronts of their lives.

One such student was Divyanshi, a shy and introverted girl who felt lost in the bustling sea of adolescence. Struggling to find her voice, she often found solace in the realm of books. Ms. Singh recognized Divyanshi's love for reading and quietly encouraged her to share her thoughts in class. As Divyanshi hesitantly began participating, the teacher's warm smile and supportive words made her feel valued.

Another student, Anjils, appeared to be a rebellious soul with a flair for mischief. Often dismissed by other teachers as a lost cause, Ms. Singh saw the potential beneath his bravado. Instead of scolding him for his antics, she engaged him in discussions about novels that dealt with themes of rebellion and personal growth. Gradually, Anjils started channelling his energy into constructive ideas, like doing theatres, and found his passion for storytelling.

The classroom soon became a melting pot of ideas, opinions, and creative expressions. Ms. Singh fostered a sense of belonging, and the students began to see each other not merely as classmates but as companions on a journey of exploration.

One afternoon, during a storytelling session, the students were asked to compose their own experiences in the form of a story. The room buzzed with pens scratching against paper, and creativity flowed like a river. Arvind, a quiet boy with a melancholic air, hesitated before presenting his story about loss and healing. As he read it aloud, tears brimmed in his eyes. The class listened in silence, touched by the raw emotion in his words. Ms. Singh offered him a gentle nod and whispered words of encouragement that stayed with him forever.

The session's harmony even extended beyond college hours. Ms. Singh organized theatres where they would discuss books, share personal stories, and enjoy each other's company. These informal gatherings strengthened the bond between the students and their teacher, creating an environment where they felt safe to open up about their fears, dreams, and insecurities.

One winter, the town experienced unexpected heavy rain with intense storms and dark clouds. Suddenly, the electricity went off due to thunderstorms and lightning, leaving the college engulfed in a blanket of darkness. Ms. Singh surprised her students by arranging an impromptu "literary torchlight." Each student was given a snippet of poetry or a quote and asked to create a metaphorical "torchlight" inspired by the text. Laughter echoed in the Lab with mobile lights as the students engaged in a friendly exchange of literary torchlight. It was a day etched in their memories, a day they realized that learning could be fun and that their teacher cared about more than just grades.

The classroom transformed into a cocoon of growth and self-discovery as the years passed. The students flourished academically and emotionally-thanks to Ms. Singh's nurturing approach. Divyanshi, who once struggled to express herself, became a confident public speaker, and she founded a book club at the local library to share her love of reading with others.

Anjils, who had embraced his passion for storytelling, published his first semi-autobiographical novel that touched readers' hearts worldwide. In his acknowledgments, he credited Ms. Singh as the one who had believed in him when nobody else did.

Arvind's story, the one he shared on that day, was published in a prestigious story anthology. His words became a source of comfort for those experiencing grief, a beacon of hope amidst darkness. He dedicated his story to Ms. Singh, acknowledging her role in helping him find his voice.

As time passed, Ms. Singh continued to be an unwavering guiding light for her students, even as they graduated and embarked on their own journeys. The bonds they had formed with her remained intact, and they often returned to visit their beloved teacher, sharing stories of their triumphs and struggles in the real world.

One summer, Ms. Singh received a WhatsApp message. It was from Aditya, a 2023 pass-out student of Information Technology. In his message, Aditya expressed his gratitude for the impact Ms. Singh had on his life. He wrote, "What we miss on our B.Tech life of four years, the learnings we had in Language Lab. You taught me not just about English and literature but also about life, love, and compassion."

Tears welled up in Ms. Singh's eyes as she read the heartfelt words. Each word was a testament to the power of connection and the significance of an educator's role in a student's life.

As the new session commenced, Ms. Singh welcomed a fresh group of eager faces into her Language Lab. She knew that this year, like every year before, would be a journey of growth, learning, and forging beautiful bonds with her students. And as she looked around at the faces before her, she couldn't wait to unravel the tapestry of words that would bind them all together.

Ms. Singh's influence reached far beyond the four walls of lab sessions. Many of her students became writers, teachers, public administrators, and advocates for education. They paid forward the gift of her guidance, touching the lives of countless others just as she had touched theirs.

Learning continues...

Triumph Over Pain and Adversity

Ananya, a beautiful girl with caramel eyes, was a promising and aspiring student of one of the most reputed central universities. Her college years were supposed to be a time of carefree exploration, late-night studies, and creating lifelong friendships. However, life had a different plan for her.

Ananya has always been an active and enthusiastic individual. Her dreams were sky-high when she took admission in the university to study literature. She wanted to become a professor and inspire generations with her love for literature. But in her first semester, as her friends were out enjoying their newfound freedom, Sophia started feeling inexplicable pain and stiffness in her joints. Simple tasks like holding a pen or even walking became agonizing.

Ananya: "Something's not right. I can barely move my fingers without pain."

Her roommate, Sarah, noticed Ananya's discomfort and concern.

Sarah: "Ananya, you should see a doctor about this. It's not normal."

After weeks of persistent pain and fatigue, Ananya sought medical advice. The diagnosis was crushing: rheumatoid arthritis, a progressive chronic autoimmune disease that often causes pain, swelling, and stiffness in the joints. Ananya was devastated. The diagnosis put her life in a different direction, making her helpless for a while.

The question that used to prick her was, "Why me?"

No one could answer this question, and she could not bear the pain she was going through.

Ananya's battle with rheumatoid arthritis was relentless. College life became a juggling act of managing her coursework, medications, and the physical challenges posed by her condition. She faced disheartening moments when she had to rely on a walking aid to get to her classes, and her friends' pitying glances were difficult to bear.

Ananya (teary-eyed): "I don't know if I can do this, guys."

Her friends, Priya and Raj, rallied around her.

Priya: "You're not alone in this, Ananya. We're here for you."

Raj: "And we'll make sure you get to all your classes, no matter what."

On the other hand, Ananya's parents were consulting doctors to find a cure for this disease, but the answer was the same, "There is no cure; the child has to accept this and adopt the lifestyle that helps in bearing the pain." Her parents did not know how to console their child.

However, Ananya's determination shone through. She sought support from the university's disability services, which provided her with accommodations such as extra time for assignments and accessible classroom seating. With unwavering tenacity, Ananya adapted her study routine, learning to use voice recognition software for typing when her fingers refused to move. She was given steroids to control the pain. She had to tune her mind to understand that she had to overcome this pain and the pain could not be the barrier to her life goals.

She religiously started following the doctor's advice, but then her fingers started deforming, and now her disease was visible to all. Everyone started noticing her and used to give different advice that deepened her agony.

Amid her struggles, Ananya found an unexpected mentor in Professor Karthik, a renowned literature professor at Shimla University. Ananya had always admired his work, and she had never imagined that she would have the opportunity to study under him.

Ananya (to Professor Karthik): "Professor Karthik, your work has always inspired me."

Professor Karthik, though tough as a teacher, recognized Ananya's potential and was deeply moved by her determination. He became more than a mentor; he was a guiding light through her darkest days. He adjusted his teaching style to accommodate Ananya's needs, providing her with recorded lectures and additional reading material to make her studies more manageable.

Ananya's friendship with Professor Karthik extended beyond the classroom. He shared stories of his own challenges and setbacks, assuring her that her dreams were still within reach. Under his guidance, Ananya learned not only about literature but also about resilience, perseverance, and the indomitable spirit of the human will.

Four years flew by, marked by moments of pain, frustration, and triumph. Ananya graduated from Shimla University with a degree in literature, but her journey was far from over. Her arthritis had left its mark, but it had not defeated her. She decided to pursue a master's degree in literature, with the ultimate goal of becoming a professor.

Ananya's journey to her master's was equally challenging, marked by late-night study sessions and flare-ups of her condition. But she persevered, with the unwavering support of her family, friends, and Professor Karthik.

Her parents started looking for a match for her who could understand her situation and was ready to accept her. Many came, but no one accepted her arthritis.

Then, a boy from a small town of Uttarakhand showed interest in her profile published on the matrimonial website. He came to meet Ananya at her home. Ananya was enrolled for PhD and usually stays at home to give more focus on her research work.

When she met Rohan, a tall and whitish man with good weight, she felt the same as the other boys who came to see her.

On that day, she draped a yellow saree with a red border. She looked stunning with her caramel eyes that struck Rohan and stole his heart.

Ananya: I hope you have read my profile on the website.

Rohan: Hmm

Ananya: I mean, you must be knowing what I am going through.

Rohan: Hmm

Ananya: Your parents know about this.

Rohan: Hmm

Ananya: Your Hmm, I don't understand

Rohan (taking Ananya's hand in his hands): I know everything and your apprehensions too. After marriage, can you prepare dough for chapatis for me?

Ananya: Hmm, if sometimes I find that challenging, we can have a dough maker.

The room is filled with laughter. They both got married. Ananya continued her research work.

Years passed, and Ananya achieved her dream of becoming a professor. She returned to the same university, not as a student battling rheumatoid arthritis but as a respected faculty member. Her life story was a testament to resilience, and it inspired her students as much as Professor Karthik had inspired her.

Ananya continued to teach and mentor students, just as she had been mentored. She made it her mission to support students facing challenges similar to hers, ensuring that they received the assistance and encouragement they needed to overcome their obstacles.

Throughout her journey, there was one unspoken battle Ananya faced. Due to the severity of her rheumatoid arthritis and the medications she had to take, she and her husband, Rohan, could not conceive a child. This was a painful reality they both had to come to terms with.

Rohan (supportive but saddened): "Ananya, I love you, and I don't want anything to come between us and our dreams."

Ananya (teary-eyed): "I know, Rohan. We'll find other ways to build our family."

Ananya's journey from a struggling college student with rheumatoid arthritis to a respected professor at university was a remarkable testament to the power of determination and the support of mentors. Her legacy extended beyond her academic achievements; it was a reminder that adversity could be conquered with unwavering resolve.

Ananya's story became an inspiration for countless others who faced physical or emotional challenges. She showed them that with the right support and an unyielding spirit, they could achieve their dreams, regardless of the obstacles in their path.

In the hallowed halls of the university, Ananya's story was a reminder that resilience could turn pain into strength and dreams could be achieved, no matter how daunting the journey. She proved that the human spirit could overcome even the most formidable challenges, leaving an indelible mark on the hearts of all who knew her. They proved that family could be built through love, support, and shared dreams.

Ananya and Rohan are now happily troubling each other; Ananya's arthritis has been in the remission period for the last 15 years and she is leading a healthy life.

The Journey of Singh's Family

The Singh family lived in the serene town of Roorkee, nestled among the lush green hills of Uttarakhand. Mr. Singh, a dedicated government servant, was the head of the family. He was married to a woman known for her unwavering strength and kind heart. Together, they were blessed with four wonderful children - two sons, Monu and Sonu, and two daughters, Dolly and Ruchi. The Singhs' home was filled with the laughter of children playing, birds singing in the trees, and the rhythmic clatter of their mother's bangles as she went about her daily chores. It was a picture of warmth and togetherness.

Mrs. Singh: (Smiling) "Our children are our greatest treasure, dear."

Mr. Singh: (Nodding) "Indeed, they are. We're a complete

family."

But life has a way of testing even the strongest of families. Mr. Singh had been experiencing persistent health issues, but he chose to bear this burden in silence, not wanting to burden his family with his worries. Months passed, and his condition worsened, but he hid it well. One day, Mr. Singh fell seriously ill. It was a diagnosis that shattered their world - multiple organ failure. The entire family rallied around him, seeking the best medical care possible.

The family's life changed dramatically one evening when Mrs. Singh received an urgent call from the hospital. Mr. Singh had taken a turn for the worse, and the doctor needed her presence immediately.

Doctor: (Serious) "Mrs. Singh, I'm afraid your husband's condition has deteriorated significantly. We've done everything we can, but it's critical that you come to the hospital right away."

Tears welled up in Mrs. Singh's eyes as she rushed to the hospital, the click-clack of her sandals echoing in the empty corridors. The sterile smell of disinfectants filled the air as she entered the ICU, where her husband lay, frail and pale.

Mrs. Singh: (Tearfully) "Doctor, please, do whatever you can to save him."

Doctor: (Gently) "We're doing our best, Mrs. Singh. But you must prepare yourself for the worst."

Mrs. Singh sat by her husband's bedside, holding his frail hand, her silent prayers filling the room. Hours turned into days as she kept her vigil, the beeping of machines and the whisper of nurses providing a backdrop to her thoughts.

One evening, as the sun dipped below the horizon, Mr. Singh turned to his wife, his voice weak but filled with love.

Mr. Singh: (Whispering) " I am grateful for the life we shared together. Please promise me, you will always be strong for our children."

Mrs. Singh: (Tears streaming down her face) "I promise. I will be their rock."

But despite lot of efforts, Mr. Singh succumbed to his illness, leaving the Singhs heartbroken.

Sonu: (Tears in his eyes) "Papa, please don't leave us."

Mrs. Singh: (Holding back tears) "We have to be strong for each other."

Relatives who had once been close turned their backs on the bereaved family, leaving them to stand for themselves in their time of need.

Meanwhile, during the same period, Monu's health had deteriorated significantly. Unable to bear the loss of his father, he was bedridden at AIIMS Delhi. An intestinal disease had struck him, necessitating a critical surgery.

After the operation, Monu's stomach remained open, requiring daily dressings and careful attention from the doctors and nurses at AIIMS Delhi. Despite the excruciating pain and the debilitating nature of his condition, Monu displayed an astonishing resilience, mirroring the strength he had seen in his parents.

Each day, the hospital room echoed with the sterile rustle of medical equipment and the gentle voices of the medical team as they attended to Monu's needs. Monu was so close to his father that at last he gave up and closed his eyes forever. It was another shock for the Singh family.

The Singhs were plunged into a world of darkness, but Mrs. Singh was not one to give in to despair. She had learned from her husband the importance of resilience and showed the strength of a mother's love.

Mrs. Singh: (Resolute) "We will make it through, no matter what."

The first challenge was to ensure that her children's education continued. Mr. Singh had always believed that education was the path to a brighter future, and she was determined to honor his memory. The scratch of pens on paper and the rustle of textbooks became the sounds of their determination. But the road ahead was far from easy. The family has started giving tuition to small children to pay school fees and on the other hand, Mrs. Singh completed the official formality for getting a pension to get regular income.

Years passed, and the Singhs' home was filled not only

with the sounds of determination but also with the sounds of success. Ruchi, with her unwavering commitment, secured a government job, stepping into her father's shoes.

Sonu, who had graduated from the prestigious IIT Roorkee, found employment in a multinational company. His achievements were a testament to the values instilled in him by his parents. Both daughters, Dolly and Ruchi, found loving partners and started their own families, just as their parents had hoped. The sounds of the Singh family's triumph echoed through the town of Roorkee, inspiring others to overcome their challenges.

In the end, it was the unwavering strength of a mother's love, the resilience of her children, and the unbreakable bonds of family that allowed the Singh family to rise above their hardships and find happiness once more. Their story served as a reminder that even in the face of adversity, the human spirit can triumph, and the echoes of hope and courage can be heard far and wide in the hills of Uttarakhand.

Divorce: The New Beginning

In the picturesque town nestled among rolling hills, five friends reigned supreme - Pooja, Gauri, Gunjan, Chhavi, and Nidhi. Their mischievous antics were legendary, and they were known for their ability to tease the boys of their society with playful nicknames. They had a secret hideaway beneath a neem tree at the back side of their society gate.

One a sunny afternoon, as they gathered under their favourite tree, Pooja, the ringleader, proposed an idea that would change their lives forever. "Let's create a place where no grown-ups can tell us what to do," she suggested with a sly grin. The girls agreed, and with determination, they began to build their secret haven. Blankets, pillows, and discarded paint cans from Gauri's garage became the raw materials for their cozy corner. It was a kaleidoscope of colours, adorned with mismatched cushions, posters of rock bands, and twinkling fairy lights. They christened it "The Land of Chatter" for a reason.

Nicknaming the boys of their society became their favourite pastime. Raj was dubbed "Mr. Smooth Talker" for his charming ways, while Vikram became "Silent Whisper" due to his shyness. Rohan, the clown, was lovingly called "Master Joker." Nobody, not even the uncles and aunts, escaped their playful nicknames. Here comes Aryan, the love of Pooja. Pooja confessed her feelings about Aryan with her friends under their favourite neem tree "The land of chatter"

"But he is already married", Pooja with a sinking heart whispered.

"He is married to Kavita. What should I do?"

Gauri put her hand on Pooja's shoulder and said, "Pooja, love is complex. But you must be honest with Aryan. If he feels the same way, he needs to decide about his marriage."

Pooja's love for Aryan was undeniable, and he too found himself drawn to her. After months of turmoil, they decided to confront their emotions and speak with Kavita.

II

Aryan couldn't bear to see Kavita in pain any longer. He knew he had to be honest with her, so one evening, he asked her to sit down for a serious conversation.

"Aryan, you seemed disturbed," Kavita said, concern in

her eyes as they sat in their cozy living room.

Aryan sighed, struggling to find the right words. "Kavita, there's something I need to tell you. It's not easy, and I hope you'll understand."

Kavita's heart skipped a beat, sensing the gravity of the situation. "What is it, Aryan? You can tell me anything."

Taking a deep breath, Aryan admitted, "I've fallen in love with someone else, Kavita. It's Pooja, one of the girls from town."

Kavita's eyes welled up with tears, and she looked away, her voice trembling. "Aryan, how could you?"

Aryan reached out and gently touched her hand. "I never meant for this to happen. It just did. I'm so sorry, Kavita."

As Kavita wiped away her tears, she asked with a quivering voice, "What do you want, Aryan? What are you saying?"

Aryan looked into Kavita's eyes, his own filled with regret. "I can't continue like this, Kavita. I want to be with Pooja. We've decided to get a divorce."

Kavita's heart sank, but she knew that fighting to hold onto a love that had already slipped away would only bring more pain. With a heavy heart, she nodded, signalling her acceptance of the inevitable.

Aryan's confession to Kavita shattered their marriage. She

couldn't bear the pain of sharing her husband and decided to file for divorce. The news sent shockwaves through the town, and gossip spread like wildfire. Pooja's friends were torn between loyalty to her and sympathy for Kavita. Their once tight-knit group was in turmoil.

As Pooja's relationship with Aryan became more serious, she knew she had to confront her family about their love, and she braced herself for their reaction.

One evening, Pooja gathered the courage to talk to her parents, Raj and Meera.

"Pooja, you seem distracted," her father Raj observed, concern evident in his voice.

Pooja took a deep breath and replied, "Dad, Mom, there's something I need to tell you, and I hope you'll understand."

Meera, her mother, exchanged a worried glance with her husband. "What's going on, Pooja? You can tell us anything."

Pooja hesitated for a moment, then confessed, "I've fallen in love with someone, and it's serious. His name is Aryan."

Raj and Meera exchanged surprised looks, and Raj finally spoke up, "Aryan? Is he from around here?"

Pooja nodded, her heart pounding in her chest. "Yes, Dad, but there's something else you should know. Aryan was married to Kavita, and they got a divorce because of us."

Meera gasped, her hands flying to her mouth in shock. "A divorce? Oh, Pooja!"

Raj's face hardened, and he demanded, "Pooja, how could you be involved in something like this? We raised you with better values."

Pooja's voice quivered as she tried to explain, "Dad, Mom, I can't help who I fell in love with. It just happened, above all Aryan and I truly love each other."

Raj's anger flared, and he said with frustration, "Love is not an excuse for breaking someone's marriage, Pooja. This is not what we expected from you."

Meera, tears in her eyes, added, "Pooja, you're our daughter, and we want the best for you. But this situation is so complicated, and it's causing pain to others."

Pooja felt a mixture of guilt and frustration. She had expected her family's discontent, but hearing it was still painful. "I know it's complicated, and I never wanted to hurt anyone. But I have to follow my heart, even if it means facing your disapproval."

The conversation weighed heavily on everyone in the room. Pooja's family struggled to come to terms with the unexpected turn of events, and Pooja knew that their discontent would continue to cast a shadow over her relationship with Aryan.

Pooja knew that she needed to talk to Kavita, Aryan's ex-wife, about her feelings and the complicated situation that had unfolded. One afternoon, she mustered the courage to reach out to her.

Pooja and Kavita decided to meet in a small, quiet café in town. As they sat across from each other, the tension in the air was palpable.

Pooja took a deep breath and began, "Kavita, I know this is incredibly difficult for both of us, but I think it's important that we talk."

Kavita, her eyes filled with a mix of sadness and anger, nodded in agreement. "I've been expecting this conversation."

Pooja continued, her voice sincere, "I didn't intend for any of this to happen. My feelings for Aryan just grew, and I can't deny them. I'm deeply sorry for the pain it's caused you."

Kavita, her voice trembling, replied, "You don't know how much it hurt to hear Aryan confess his feelings for you. Our marriage, our life together, shattered in an instant."

Tears welled up in Pooja's eyes as she said, "I can't even begin to imagine what you're going through, Kavita. I wish there was something I could do to make it right."

Kavita sighed and said, "I appreciate your honesty, Pooja. But it doesn't change the fact that my life has been upended because of this. I loved Aryan deeply."

Pooja nodded, her own emotions raw. "I know you loved him, and I'm sorry that I've caused you so much pain."

Kavita took a moment to collect her thoughts before saying, "I've decided to file for divorce. I can't hold onto a marriage when it's clear that Aryan's heart is with you."

Pooja's heart sank at Kavita's words, realizing the gravity of the situation. "I never wanted it to come to this, Kavita. Please know that I didn't set out to break your marriage."

Kavita looked into Pooja's eyes, her anger softening into resignation. "I believe you, Pooja. Love can be unpredictable. Just promise me you'll take care of Aryan."

Pooja nodded, tears streaming down her face, and whispered, "I promise, Kavita. I'll do my best to make him happy."

Their conversation was laden with pain and understanding. They both knew that their lives had been forever changed by the twists of fate and now they had to navigate the difficult path ahead with grace and compassion.

In the aftermath of her divorce from Aryan and the emotional turmoil that followed, Kavita knew she needed to find a way to heal and move forward with her life. It was a daunting task, but she was determined to embrace a new beginning.

One sunny morning, Kavita sat by the window in her

small, cozy apartment, sipping a cup of tea. The warm sunlight streamed in, and a sense of hope began to replace the darkness of the past.

As she looked around at her surroundings, Kavita realized that she had a chance to rediscover herself. She decided to start by pursuing her long-neglected passions. Kavita had always loved painting, but it had taken a backseat during her marriage. Now, she purchased a canvas and some paints, and she began to pour her emotions onto the canvas.

Each stroke of the brush became a form of therapy for Kavita. The vibrant colours and intricate details mirrored her journey from heartache to healing. She soon joined a local art class, where she made new friends and discovered the joy of creating art once more.

Kavita also found solace in writing. She began a journal to document her thoughts and feelings, allowing herself to process the pain and betrayal she had experienced. Over time, her journal transformed into a blog where she shared her journey of recovery and self-discovery. Her candid writing resonated with others who had faced similar challenges, and she realized that her words could offer comfort and inspiration.

As she reconnected with her passions and embarked on a journey of self-care, Kavita's self-esteem began to grow. She started attending therapy sessions, which helped her gain a better understanding of herself and her needs. With the support of her therapist, she slowly rebuilt her confidence and self-worth.

Kavita also rekindled old friendships and formed new ones. Her friends rallied around her, providing a strong support system during her most difficult moments. Together, they explored new hobbies, went on adventures, and celebrated small victories.

Over time, Kavita's outlook on life began to change. She realized that her divorce, while painful, had also been a catalyst for personal growth. She had emerged from the ashes of a broken marriage stronger and more resilient. She understood that her happiness was no longer dependent on her relationship status.

Kavita's new beginning was marked by a sense of empowerment and self-discovery. She had learned to find happiness within herself and was excited about the opportunities that lay ahead. As she continued to embrace her passions, nurture her friendships, and focus on her well-being, Kavita's life blossomed into a beautiful tapestry of resilience and renewal.

The Slippers

Mahi and Rudra, two siblings, were known throughout the neighborhood for their boundless energy and mischievous spirits. Their mother, Nikita, however, had a secret weapon to keep them in line – her old slippers. The slippers had been through countless adventures of motherhood.

Nikita's slippers were more than an article of clothing. They were a symbol of her maternal strength and the warmth of her home. They carried with them the echoes of children's laughter, the whispers of bedtime stories, and the unspoken language of a mother's love. Through their unpretentious simplicity, they told a story of timeless devotion and the enduring bond between a mother and her family.

One evening, the atmosphere in Nikita's household was filled with a mixture of tension and laughter. It was study time for Rudra, and he was engaged in a heated discussion with his elder sister, Mahi, on the bicycle that he wanted as his birthday gift.

Nikita, who had been busy in the kitchen, decided it was time to intervene.

Nikita (calling out): Rudra, dear, it's study time now. Mahi is helping you, so do focus.

But when the argument continued, she stepped into the living room, clutching her weapon, an old slipper, with a mischievous smile. Her plan was to toss it playfully in Rudra's direction as a signal to get back to work. Nikita (smiling): Time to bring out Mama's secret weapon!

With a dramatic flourish, Nikita tosses the slipper towards Rudra. But, to everyone's shock, it veers off course, propelled by an unseen force or perhaps Nikita's overzealous aim, and flies straight through the open window.

Nikita (in disbelief): Oh no!

The slipper sails through the window with surprising speed, disappearing from sight. Mahi and Rudra watch in stunned silence.

Mahi (wide-eyed): Mom, did you see that?

Rudra (gulping): Uh-oh, where did it go?

Their words are cut short by a sudden commotion from

outside. Shouts and surprised exclamations fill the air.

Voice from outside (shouting): Hey! What just hit me?

Mahi and Rudra rush to the window and peep outside, their eyes widening in realization. Nikita's trusty old slipper has hit their neighbor, Mr. Sharma, who was innocently tending to his garden.

Mr. Sharma (holding up the slipper): Well, I never expected to get hit by a flying slipper today!

Mahi, Rudra, and Nikita exchange alarmed glances, and Nikita quickly rushes outside to retrieve her slipper.

Nikita (mortified): Mr. Sharma, I am so sorry! It was meant for Rudra!

Mr. Sharma, a good-humored neighbor, chuckles and hands the slipper back to Nikita.

Mr. Sharma (grinning): Well, I'll be the talk of the neighborhood now, won't I? Your slipper really knows how to make an entrance!

II

It had been years, and Rudra, now a grown man, found himself reminiscing about his mother's slipper long after his marriage. The slipper, which had once been a source of playfulness and laughter in his childhood, was now a tangible connection to his mother who had passed away after a long battle with cancer.

One evening, as Rudra and his wife, Aarti, sat in their living room, surrounded by the warmth of family photographs and mementos, Rudra found himself sharing stories of his mother with a contemplative smile.

Rudra: You know, Aarti, there's something I've never told you about. It's my mother's slipper.

Aarti: Your mother's slipper? What's the story behind it?

Rudra: Well, it's a long story, but it's special to me. My mother used to playfully use it to discipline us when we were kids. She was such a loving and caring woman, and that slipper was like a symbol of her motherly authority.

Aarti: That sounds like a unique and heartwarming tradition.

Rudra: It was, indeed. Even after all these years, I still have those slippers. They are kept safely in the attic. Sometimes, when I miss her, I take it out, and it's like she's right here with me.

Aarti: It's a way of keeping her memory alive.

Rudra: (emotionally) Yes, exactly. It's more than just a slipper; it's a connection to the wonderful woman she was. She taught me so much about life, love, and laughter. And that slipper... it's like a reminder of her playful side, even in adversity.

As the evening continued, Rudra and Aarti reminisced

about the past, sharing stories of their families and the values they held dear. The slipper, though a simple object, became a symbol of the enduring love Rudra held for his mother and a testament to the way her legacy continued to shape his life.

The Puppet

Priya, a 12-year-old girl, was a bright-eyed, curious child with an innate talent for creating puppets. Every day, as the golden rays of the morning sun streamed through the cracks in their modest mud-walled hut, Priya could be found sitting on a worn-out rug beside her mother, Kanta. Kanta was Priya's guiding light and her partner in puppetry. Together, they transformed bits of colourful cloth, twine, and buttons into enchanting puppets with intricate details. Each puppet had its own unique character and charm, and Priya poured her boundless creativity into every stitch. As Priya's nimble fingers worked alongside her mother's experienced hands, their home echoed with laughter and the soft rustling of fabric. Kanta would share stories of her childhood, tales of wonder and adventure that transported Priya to far-off lands and magical realms.

Priya's favourite part of their puppet-making ritual was choosing the names for their creations. She'd give them names like "Sundar," meaning beautiful, for the puppets with vibrant, flowing garments, and "Buddhi," meaning wise, for those with thoughtful expressions. But her dearest puppet, whom she always kept beside her, was named "Madhav." Madhav had a twinkle in his button eyes and an air of quiet wisdom that drew Priya's heart. Every evening, as the sun dipped below the horizon and the world outside faded into twilight, Priya would gather her beloved puppets around her. Madhav, with his air of wisdom, always took centre stage. She would weave stories of enchantment and wisdom, using Madhav to convey the profound life lessons she had learned from her mother.

As the villagers learned of Priya's talent for puppetry, they began to gather outside her home, drawn by the magical tales she wove. The puppets came to life in her skilled hands, captivating young and old alike. The small village, often untouched by the outside world, found solace and inspiration in Priya's stories. Yet, the village was not without its challenges. The caste system cast long shadows over the lives of its residents, and Priya's family belonged to a low caste that traditionally faced discrimination and limited opportunities. The villagers, though enchanted by Priya's stories, were bound by tradition, and many believed that a girl like Priya should focus on her chores and eventually marry a suitable partner from their caste.

Rajaram returned from the fields one fateful evening and found the Zamindar's representatives waiting for him.

They delivered a stern message filled with thinly veiled threats. The Zamindar had heard about Priya's pursuit of education and her involvement in puppetry, and he was deeply displeased. "You must control your daughter," the representatives warned Rajaram. "These pursuits are not suitable for a girl of her caste. She must stay within the confines of your home, and you must consider finding her a suitable husband soon. It is not in your best interest to defy the Zamindar."

Rajaram's heart sank as he listened to the ominous message. He knew that defying the Zamindar's wishes could have disastrous consequences for their entire family. The Zamindar held immense power and influence over their lives, and any act of rebellion would likely result in the loss of their home, their livelihood, and their safety. Torn between his love for Priya and the fear of punishment from the Zamindar, Rajaram had no choice but to make an agonizing decision. He called Priya to their small, dimly lit hut, where the flickering lantern barely illuminated their faces. With tears in his eyes, he explained the situation and the danger that loomed over them. "I cannot bear to see you suffer, my dear Priya," he said, his voice trembling with emotion. "We are bound by circumstances beyond our control. For your safety and the well-being of our family, you must stay within these four walls, and we must consider finding you a husband soon. It breaks my heart to do this, but I see no other choice."

Though devastated by her father's words, Priya understood the gravity of the situation. She knew the world outside their home was filled with prejudice and danger. Reluctantly, she agreed to comply with her father's wishes, her dreams of education and puppetry temporarily set aside. The decision weighed heavily on Rajaram's heart. He knew it was a painful sacrifice made out of love and fear, and he couldn't help but feel a deep sense of powerlessness in the face of the Zamindar's authority. As the days turned into weeks, Priya's world grew smaller. She could no longer sneak away to the banyan tree to study and practice puppetry. Instead, she spent her days within the confines of their home, her dreams and aspirations hidden away like the secrets in her heart.

Burdened by the weight of his decision, Rajaram continued to labour in the fields, doing everything in his power to ensure the safety and well-being of his beloved daughter. All the while, the village continued to buzz with the stifling expectations of conformity, leaving Priya to wonder if there would ever be a path to freedom and fulfilment beyond the walls of their home. However, Priya's dreams stretched far beyond the confines of her village. She yearned for an education, the chance to learn about the world beyond her home, and the opportunity to share her puppetry and stories with a wider audience. Her parents, especially her father, Rajaram, found themselves torn between the love for their daughter and the weight of tradition. The villagers began to whisper about Priya's unfulfilled potential, and the idea of her early marriage loomed ever closer.

One day, as Priya sat in the dimly lit corner of her small hut, her hands idly holding Madhav, her favourite puppet, a spark of inspiration ignited. She looked at Madhav's wise, twinkling eyes and felt a surge of determination. Perhaps, she thought, Madhav could help her find a way to pursue her dreams even within the confines of her home. With renewed hope, Priya began to craft a plan. She spent hours talking to Madhav as if the puppet were her confidant and advisor. She whispered her dreams, fears, frustrations, and hopes into Madhav's ear. In Priya's mind, the puppet became a symbol of wisdom and guidance, a trusted friend who would help her find a way. With his seemingly magical insight, Madhav soon became the central character in Priya's puppetry shows. She developed stories where Madhav, the wise and resourceful puppet, encountered challenges similar to hers but always found ingenious ways to overcome them. These stories served a dual purpose - they entertained the villagers and conveyed important lessons about resilience and determination. As Priya's puppetry shows gained popularity, the villagers began to see her talent in a new light. They were drawn to the wisdom and creativity of Madhav, and slowly, the prejudices that had once confined Priya began to weaken. People from different castes and backgrounds attended her shows, and the once-staunch opposition to her education and aspirations began to waver.

Word of Priya's puppetry shows and the remarkable character of Madhav reached even the Zamindar's ears. He, too, attended one of Priya's performances, curious to see what had captivated the villagers. As he watched Madhav's clever solutions to various challenges, a subtle change came over him. The power of storytelling and the wisdom conveyed through puppetry began to soften his heart. After the performance, the Zamindar approached

Priya and her father. He was still stern, but his eyes showed a glimmer of understanding. "Your puppetry is quite extraordinary," he admitted. "It seems that even in the face of adversity, one can find a way to shine."

Encouraged by the Zamindar's words, Priya seized the opportunity to speak with him. With confidence and grace, she explained her passion for education and her dream of a brighter future not only for herself but for all the children in the village. She spoke of the transformative power of knowledge and how her puppetry had bridged gaps and brought people together. The Zamindar, influenced by both Priya's words and Madhav's wisdom, found himself moved by her sincerity and determination. After a thoughtful pause, he made a surprising decision. "I will support your education," he said, "and I will ensure that other children in the village have access to it as well." Priya and her father were astonished by the Zamindar's unexpected generosity. It was a turning point that allowed Priya to pursue her education openly, and she continued to use her puppetry and storytelling to inspire change and promote learning in the village.

The Jerk

The night was draped in darkness as Richa lay in her childhood bedroom, her face bathed in the cold glow of the moon. The room was a time capsule, preserving the memories of a life once filled with dreams and aspirations. Tonight, those dreams would return, more haunting and vivid than ever before. As the clock ticked past midnight, Richa found herself lost in a deep slumber. In the recesses of her subconscious, the dream unfolded like a malevolent ghost. She stood before an operating table, wearing a sterile white coat. Her gloved hands held a scalpel, and her gaze was locked onto the lifeless body of a rat sprawled out in front of her. The smell of formaldehyde stung her nostrils. But this was no ordinary rat. It was the embodiment of her childhood dreams, her passion for the intricate art of dissection. Richa had always known she wanted to be a surgeon, to heal and save lives. The precision of her cuts, and the way she navigated the intricate anatomy, had always set her apart.

As Richa began to make the first incision, the rat's tiny, glassy eyes seemed to stare into her soul, accusing her of abandoning her dreams. But before she could complete the procedure, a sudden jerk, like a bolt of lightning, shook her awake.

Richa gasped as she jolted upright in bed. Her heart raced, and beads of sweat dotted her forehead. The room was creepily silent, saved for the rhythmic ticking of the clock. It had been years since she had experienced the dream that had haunted her ever since she lost her father during her final board exams. The day of the exams had been etched into her memory like scar. Her father, her biggest supporter and the one who had shared her dream of becoming a surgeon had passed away suddenly because of multiple organ failure. The grief had engulfed her, and she had abandoned her dreams to take care of her grieving family.

The jerk that had awakened her at night was a cruel reminder of the life she had left behind. The dream, with its vivid imagery of dissecting rats, had resurfaced with a vengeance, taunting her with the echoes of her unfulfilled aspirations. Richa knew she had to confront her past and the dreams she had buried. The memory of her father, with his unwavering belief in her abilities, gave her the courage to revisit her long-abandoned passion.

One day, Richa received an unexpected offer that would change the course of her life. Her maternal uncle, who had always believed in her potential, offered her a choice. She could stay with his family and join a Bachelor of Science program, majoring in biology. It was a chance to immerse herself in her beloved field once more. With a mixture of excitement and apprehension, Richa accepted her uncle's offer.

Richa embarked on her journey to her uncle's city, filled with hope and determination. However, upon arriving, she quickly realized that her struggles were far from over. Her uncle's family, while supportive of her education, had their own demands and responsibilities.

With three daughters and a medically challenged son, Suhash, to care for, Richa found herself burdened with household chores and caregiving responsibilities. Her dreams of immersing herself in her studies and becoming a skilled surgeon were slipping further away with each passing day. It appeared that this so-called mama's family had asked her to help manage the household, putting her dreams of higher education and a fulfilling career on hold.

One day, as the weight of her responsibilities became almost unbearable, Richa called her mother. She poured her heart out, sharing the true extent of her situation at her maternal uncle's house. Hearing the agony in her daughter's voice, her mother felt a mixture of concern and determination. It was unbelievable for her, but the fact is that nobody keeps someone's child. She realized that the world is cruel and demands things in return; even the relatives turn their faces in times of adversity. She decided to keep all her children together and asked Richa to come home, and then together, they would decide as she could not see her child working as a servant just because her father was no longer with her. This incident shook her, and then she started making decisions with the consent of her children without any interference or suggestions from others or relatives.

Richa returned to her home and joined a private college, her dream of a medical career all over, and now she wanted to be with her family. She pursued her graduation with renewed determination, not in biology, but in English Literature. During this time, she honed her teaching skills, sharing her knowledge with classmates and helping them excel in their studies. As she completed her post-graduation, Richa found herself drawn to the world of academia. Her passion for teaching had grown, and she decided to continue her studies, eventually earning her Ph.D. in English Literature. It was a remarkable journey of self-discovery, resilience, and an unwavering commitment to her own growth.

Armed with her Ph.D. and a wealth of teaching experience, Richa's journey had come full circle. She was appointed as faculty at a prestigious Government Engineering College. While her career had taken an unexpected turn, it was a path that had led her to a place of fulfillment she had never imagined. Richa's classroom was now filled with eager engineering students, and her teaching skills had blossomed into a true art form. She had become a mentor, an inspiration, and a guide to young minds eager to learn and grow.

Richa's life had taken a different path than the one she had initially envisioned, but it had been a path of purpose and fulfillment. Her teaching skills, developed during her time of hardship, had become the cornerstone of her successful career as an educator. She had become a healer in her own right, touching lives with words and wisdom, just as her father had believed she could. And in that classroom, she had finally found the fulfillment and contentment that had eluded her for so long.